Foreword

The Sister Dora award for Cultural Diversity was presented to the Black Reading Group by Noddy Holder in 2003 and on the same evening the group were finalists in the Cultural Development category. The Black Reading Group were also highly commended for the Annual Citizen Impact award in 2004 by the Chief Executive, Annie Shepherd, of Walsall Metropolitan Borough Council. The host for the evening was Nick Owen from the BBC.

The most recent nomination for the group (so far) was in October 2004 where the Black Reading Group were finalists in the category for the STAR Diversity award. This prestigious event was hosted by Kay Alexander from the BBC.

The Black Reading Group would like to thank from the bottom of their hearts all the lovely team at Forward Press, particularly Ian Walton, whom they call the 'Good Samaritan'. They would like to mention and thank Kerrie Pateman (Communications Manager), Mark Rainey (Design Manager), and the editors, Sarah Marshall and Chiara Cervasio. They all have been a tower of strength for the group.

Contents

The Authors

Doreen Barrett

She was born in Jamaica. She came to England in 1966 to join her mom and dad and 2 younger sisters. She arrived in England on a cold and frosty December morning with her sister, Audrey.

She said that her situation was similar to those of many young people in the late 1950s and 1960s whose parents came to England for better opportunities, leaving their offspring in the care of grandparents.

Doreen Barrett is a teacher in Walsall. She has 2 children. She enjoys reading, art and keep-fit as well as going to the theatre.

Me, Me Sister And We Grip

Dressed in green chiffon dress with plaited hair, my sister and I, holding hands, boarded the large BOAC 747. I can vaguely remember saying goodbye to our aunts and uncles and a reluctant grandpa and grandma. It took some persuading for Grandpa to leave his 'land' and donkey to say goodbye. We were young and did not understand the significance of our journey. The furthest we had travelled was twenty miles to stay with our uncle Dan in 'country' - and six miles to the next district to see our paternal grandma and aunts. But why was Grandpa just chewing on his tobacco, scratching his head and not talking to us? He normally had a hug for us, and then threw us over his shoulder.

He had already lost a favourite daughter and son to that big bird in the sky. He knew the pattern of events and perhaps realised that it would be several years before he would set eyes on us again. He had after all raised us two girls without parents as his own - one of whom had not even set eyes on her father: a 'pupa' who had not cuddled or stroked her hair. This young girl was chiselled in the way of her grandpa: a fiery temper, self-assured and cantankerous.

At the top of the stairs we giggled, turned and waved goodbye to our relatives. Not long after we found our seats. I remember a fair skinned lady dressed in navy and red came to fasten us in.

My recollection of that long journey through night and day is shaky, though I distinctly remember my first meal in the sky, using small plastic trays with food that looked and tasted unusual to me. I liked the shiny silver knife, fork and spoons. These were to be part of my life for over twenty years: the fair skinned lady had mistakenly dropped some of the cutlery when clearing away and I took the spoon and fork with the BOAC crest and slipped them into my plaited and floral straw bag. This memento later followed me to college and into early married life, a symbol of that long, dark journey.

The journey took us through America. I remember disembarking and being shuffled into a large room with other passengers. We were sternly instructed not to leave the building, anyone doing so would be arrested. To get to the large room we had to navigate the 'moving staircase'. We had not seen one of these before and my sister and I stood for a very long time trying to work out how we were to get on. We watched as others held on to the rail and jumped on. We waited and waited then jumped on holding hands. We were allowed to use the toilet; again this was foreign to me. In the yard we did not have the luxury of an indoor toilet or shower. We all shared a communal shower and wooden pit toilet. My sister and I huddled together in a corner on the floor, the cold night air flowing through my thin dress, my plaits becoming ruffled and untidy. The long wait was beginning to wear us down.

My thoughts drifted to what was to come, a strange land and people who I had only read or heard about: my mother and father were images in a frame, my new sisters known only through photographs. I wondered what they were like. Would I like them? Would they like my sister and I? Would the earth be smooth and white, or hard and rocky like my yard? Would I be able to walk barefooted or would it be cold like the snowballs we often bought to quench our thirst?

There were many adults around us talking, smoking and ignoring us. No one spoke to us; no one seemed to notice the two little girls huddled together in the corner. Torchlight helped us to board the big bird for the last part of the journey. From time to time I would lift the blind and stare into the darkness. I had no sense of excitement or anticipation at meeting my 'new family'.

I felt miserable at the family that I had left behind and the familiar scenes. I remembered our last day skipping in the yard playing with friends and cousins who were soon to be replaced. Our games were simple and repetitive; squeals and laughter as we jumped high to avoid being caught. Day turned into evening. I went into the house to find my aunt and grandmother packing the remainder of things into our grip. They argued over the fried fish and roasted breadfruit; should they be wrapped into another layer of brown paper? Was there enough to go round? The red sorrel drink would burst and ruin the clothes, but they were sure that the drink would be welcomed, as they could not get such things in England. The gifts for relatives outnumbered the measly possessions that I was to take with me. I remembered a pink skinned doll with white tight curls, which was sent to me from England, being packed and the arguments whether I needed to take it with me as I would soon be able to get another one; if it was removed it would make way for the Christmas cake. My doll remained and the rum soaked cake was wrapped several times in brown paper and squashed in before the grip was closed. The shiny keys were placed in the plaited bag that I was to carry by hand with several reminders not to lose it.

I was eager to be reunited with my uncle. He had not long made a similar journey. I remembered the days when he used to take me to school; the long walks through the woods to the slow meandering river where we swam. I remembered his 'destructive' and inquisitive nature. The dismantling of the brown wireless to see how it worked. The loud and never-ending rows with my grandpa - my grandmother being the peacemaker - the squabbling with his brothers and sisters, the accusations that he was the favoured one. It was the pointed face and jolly nature of my uncle that I longed to see, to have him lift me on his shoulder and call my name.

We landed at Heathrow on a cold frosty December morning. As I walked across the tarmac to the arrival lounge, my sister and I clutching each other from fear of falling on the slippery surface. The fresh wind lapped my cheeks and the cold froze my lips. My green chiffon dress offered no protection and was from another land and time. The arrival lounge was huge and noisy; hundreds of people vying for the attention of their loved ones. I began to panic. Would they remember that we were coming? Would someone be there to meet us? Would they recognise us? I had no idea what my mum and dad looked like. They spotted us. Three men and one woman walked towards us. One of the men I knew was my uncle, the other must be my dad, and the third was a stranger. The woman must be my mother, but how different they looked from the photographs.

We were ushered through various doors. My sister and I were still holding each other, panic and nervousness filling my empty stomach. We were told to move towards a large carousel to collect our luggage. I stared in amazement at the carousel move slowly. I couldn't remember what my grip looked like. My dad looked at the labels and eventually I was reunited with my grip to start my new life in a new country and a new family.

Untitled

Dark faces,
Young faces,
Old faces,
Shiny faces,
Many scared and wrinkled.
Bodies crouched, huddled together on scorched earth.
Weary limbs, pitiful eyes
Arms move slowly now and then to swat flies.
Bodies alive with misery.
Hunger and disease.
Suffering running through their veins.
Suffering inflicted by man, not nature.
How much more can they endure?
This terrible torture.

Sheri Barrett

She is 9 years old and is a pupil at Leighswood Primary School in Aldridge. She likes horse riding and dancing. She has lessons in ballroom, Latin and disco dancing. She has also started to learn to play the flute and recorder. Sheri enjoys arts and crafts and writing poems and stories. She also has one older brother.

The Wild Winds Of The West

Soft baby blue skies, white fluffy clouds,
Gentle breezes,
Calm winds,
A pleasant summer's day!
An outrageous roar,
A flash of lightning,
Grey clouds replaced white and blue,
A rumble of thunder . . .
War strikes the west and the east.
Water, water, plenty of it,
Gushing through the streets
Wind and water fighting
Dark skies,
Think of that
A summer's day.

Black Reading Group

Dillon Clarke

Dillon Clarke was born in 1969 and disabled after contracting TB meningitis in 1997. He spent 3 months in a coma and when he woke up he could hardly remember his name; however, he could still write. He spent 6 months in hospital and left in a wheelchair and told by doctors that he would never walk again. He said: 'Praise God I'm alive and walking now. I have lived to share my experiences and God's mercy towards me.'

Here are some of his poems.

School

I've met a lot of gangsters
Most of whom were fools.
The most dangerous gangsters I've known
Are those who learnt in school.

To learn your sums
To write and read,
Isn't up for discussion
If you want to succeed.

You may not like your tutor
But who really does?
I can't remember a teacher
Who I really loved.

On leaving school,
There's a lot I didn't get.
Because I played around,
Turned up late,
If I could be bothered,
To get out of bed.

If you're wise and not a fool,
You would have heard what I have said.
Then hopefully with constant prayer,
You won't look back with any regret.

Help

Drugs are destroying as quick as we blink.
Time doesn't matter it becomes extinct.
Before you know it the whole day's gone.
Empty pocket, feeling horrific,
Though while you inhaled you felt so terrific.
Up in smoke went your money and plastic.
Your families are hurting but will you stop it?
What started out as fun, has become an epidemic.
Where did we go wrong? Does society produce addicts?
Or is it more sinister like orchestrated magic?
Now it's too late and the government's started to panic.
Not just in Britain but all over the planet.
We're all fighting a battle for our very lives.
If not for our own, then for someone else's child.

Oxo

Recipe For Life

Add some spice to your cooking
Add some spice to your life,
Take away the stress and worry
Add a little rice if you like.

A whole barrel of liquid happy
Two dozen pleasure holidays,
With a loaf of brown prosperity
Two packets of good health
With a tin of pure sincerity.

Squeeze a bunch of loves
But squeeze them very lightly,
We've almost reached the end so listen very keenly
Before I forget, better mention on how you make your pastry.

A tiny sprinkle of flour,
With three sacks full of pure trinity
Overwhelming cupfuls of truth
Then kneed it very slowly.

Add your toppings
Spread as you like
Then place it in the oven,
But not too high.

Moderately cook
Taste if you like
Then present yourself,
In the restaurant of life.

Sonia Dixon

Sonia Dixon is an African and Caribbean Services Manager for Walsall Libraries. She was born in Birmingham, UK, and has worked for many years in Birmingham Libraries (to include Sutton Coldfield Libraries) before joining Walsall borough libraries.

After graduating in Librarianship in 1994, she was told that she was the first black person in Birmingham to become chartered in librarianship in 1995. As part of her module and exam at degree level, she looked at black writing and black authors, which she has now taken to another level where she manages and runs a Black Reading Group.

Sonia is a member of the Chartered Institute of Library and Information Professionals, and is also a member of the Performance Rights Society. She has had poetry published and a new gospel song published in the USA (2004) called 'There's nothing sweeter'. Sonia enjoys singing, the arts and speaks French and Spanish. She also finds people fascinating because she said, 'People make the world go round. Our planet is so very interesting'.

Fear

Why the rage?
Why the craze?
This has left me quite amazed
People swearing, shocking hate
Fighting in a cruel fate
Which will leave them in a state
Some may die, then it's too late.
All this blame will carry shame
On the ones who love the game.
Moaning, screaming, stamping, bleeding
Never will I have the feeling
To leave home -
I am appealing . . .
Football can be fun -
Reveal it!

Lord, With You It Is Daylight

Lord, with You it is daylight
The sunshine of my life
With all my self-deception
Just torn to one side
I pray for my repentance
A clarity that's pure
I reach for salvation
In our Saviour Jesus Lord

Those hours of enlightenment
Have trembled in my heart
I cannot give up hope now
You have promised a new start
Will You hold me forever?
Will I always feel akin?
Reaching up to Heaven
I have almost entered in

I cometh unto You, Lord
You will not cast me out
I'm a sinner and a pauper
A prisoner there's no doubt
Please save me and protect me
Be near me evermore
You're the love that I need, Lord
And the one I've waited for.

Walsall Central Library (Ethinic Services Team)
where Sonia Dixon works.

Sharon Jackson Evans

But A Coulda Whah Dat? BiBi

Bibi a get ready fi guh dunga market fi buy one or two tings fi cook. From when she see di sun a shine Bibi start fi fling out har summa clothes dem fi put on.

Mek me gi yuh de measurement ah Bibi suh unnu get de whole pichtah. Bibi did fat yuh hear nuh mek nom baddy tell yuh any different. She suppost to wear contact lenses but true sey ah bredren a foreign sen har sunglasses she a wear de national health glasses. Har hair now, come in like fowl babby gone bad an tun upside down har teet dem buff out like Concorde a tek off. Den har clothes now, well mle know sey if amen fi mi frrien me would a mek she knows sey she nuff fi badda cum out dress suh.

Bibi put on a piece a orange batty ryda it crease up inna har 40 ton batty and de belt part fasen unda har big barrel belly. De yellow top did so tieght it flatten de titti dem suh til dem reach har waise. Well me tink is har waise.

Yes man. Bibi step out pon de road wid she white habble shoes, neva mind bout traffic blockin, ere cums de endangered species. Bibi mek a stop de belly, de batty and de junjo weave bubble to de opposite direction fi gravity.

Marsa Telford from de carna shop bline as a bat, mossey call tu de cellulite queen.

'Gwan gal a yuh ave it, what a way yuh look nice, yuh nah com buy from me? Me ave a sweet long plantain fi gi yuh.'

'Missa T yuo mout too sweet fi me, yuh know sey me love melon,' Bibi replied den she rush de shop door.

'Feel ow me melon dem saff.'

'Lard god Miss Bibi me feelin kinda faint,' Marse Telford rust to de back a de shop like when hurricane a pass through.

'Me soon come,' Bibi shout waving har han den she buss de carna.

De people dem who dun mash up dem car at de traffic light de a mek on whole heep a noise fa Bibi create more excitement when she benn ova fi gi di crowd a ten pound a lard from har ryda sharts. Miss Maples de nosey Christian woman jus a cum from choir practise wid did pastor a mek dem way home dem ketch up fi see de commotion.

'Is what a gwan?' she whispered to de pastor.

Marse Telford shout out, 'De lard only mek she one,' pointing to the direction of Bibi.

Miss Maples turn round an bawl out, 'Butt kiss me **** but a could a wha dat?'

My Journey

Today I've come to the conclusion that I am going to check Bibi. My days in Jamaica, land of milk and honey were severely numbered. Outside, the number 9 bus shuttles past. The ants scampered from the cramp shutter doors heading left, right, racing towards narrow alleys and crowded streets.

'10 dallar box juice, 10 dallar box juice,' screams the little weazel, deadly with his fingers was this box juice seller. Cool, but shady with his Cheshire cat grins he pushes the scrunched up box to my face. Glittering are his knashers, brighter than clothes washed in Bold. His pegs reflected from the god, bless light that sparkled without mercy. The air was volumed with ringing from drivers yelling from street vendors. Bob Marley's greatest hits plays harmonious with the smell of Sunday best. Woo Jamaica sweet. I fanned away the little cretin.

'Move away from me,' I held my head high.

The little Judas sucked his teeth and struggled away with his broken-down cart. My slow pace had now plucked up into a 'be-bop look at me swing'. My bumper was high. 'Hello sar Jamaica nice.' I was near to Bibi's cockroach infected hideout when I was approached by a two legged joncrow fluttering behind me looking like any antique roadshow, ranstid like the pits of BO with a baby smile. I thought. How does he chew?

'Wha pen my girl?' said the whittish skinned beanpole. 'Is it me you're looking for?'

Oh my god Lionel Richie's song had been brought back from the dead.

'I can see it in your eyes,' he dribbles. 'I can 'slurp' your smile his top was not saturated. But first I must 'slurp' you.'

Another bus comes along. The dust from the gravel sweeps like a thrown blanket on our faces. I cough the near to death joncrow's mouth opens and closes 'eeyak' he looked like he was tasting it. He smirks at me with his popeye grin.

The ants outside now scatter when they see Bibi's door crack open. I mounted the gate straddling my feet either side. Bibi steps through the door. Her nostrils separate on seeing Lionel Richie's grandfather, who was about to hit the chorus. Bibi waved her hand after him.

Black Reading Group

'A wheh de half dead granny mouth, washbasin on tap a go? Move from here and gwan back a Mildred.'

A century passed before Gramps went away. I almost felt sorry for him. His clothes were not exciting at all . . . name, brand . . . extinct. Footwear . . . seen betta days just like him . . . past his sell by date. Bibi wrenched my arm.

'Look ere, Miss man deh a look a new sex kitten. Ketch im gums de dribble dribble an de splutta, guess what de las crocusbag dead from? Death by drowning.'

I folded from the gate, crossed my legs like an ostrich and laughed until I was weak. This is just the beginning of my journey and I know there's more in store to come.

Black Reading Group

Alison Graham

Alison Graham was born and brought up in County Durham. After graduating in 1966 she went to Laos as an English teacher and said that she learnt far more than she ever taught in the five years that she lived there. She was also fortunate enough to travel widely in South East Asia during the school holidays. The friends that she made and the experiences totally changed her view of the world, especially her understanding of Europe and America's colonial and imperial history.

She eventually settled in the West Midlands where her son and daughter, now grown up, were born. Her children's father is a Charlestown Maroon and readers will be aware of how profoundly her identity as their mother colours her writing. She hopes that she has enabled them to grow up proud and confident of their Jamaican heritage. She feels that in a sense all her work is for her children, whether it is the content of her writing or her commitment as a teacher to promote social justice and understanding of our common humanity. She goes on to say that she has to make whatever small contribution to our society to make it better or at least less racist for her own children and everyone else's children.

Back Home

Angela is a little girl. She lives with her mum and big sister Mary and little brother Anthony, in a house with a green door near a big park.

Her dad lives not far away in a flat of his own. Angela likes it when he comes to their house, especially when he's feeling happy.

He kisses her and Anthony and Mary and Mum. He picks her up and lifts her above his head and touches her back on the ceiling. He swings her over and round and round. He gives Mary and Anthony a turn. He puts on a tape or a record and dances with them.

'I'm so happy,' he says. 'My gladbag is bursting.'

Sometimes he goes into the kitchen. He likes to cook the dinner, but he makes it too peppery for Angela and Anthony doesn't like the peas in rice and peas. But all three children love it when he does banana or plantain fritters with bits of crispy bacon.

Sometimes they all catch a bus and go to Darkling Woods. It's fun to collect chestnuts or conkers or acorns. They like to watch the birds and listen to them as well. Once they saw a fox.

But sometimes when Dad comes he's angry and bad-tempered. He talks to Mum about what has made him angry - things in the newspapers or things that have happened to him or people have been rude and nasty. Often he looks out of the window for ages without speaking. Or reads, or watches telly or lies on the floor with his eyes wide open, saying nothing. Angela hates it when he's like that. One day he was horrible to her mum and she was really frightened.

'Never mind,' said Mum, after he had gone, 'let's go in the park.'

They walked through the trees, over the bridge and along the path to the see-saw. Angela and Anthony sat one at each end and Mary stood in the middle.

'See-saw, Margery Daw,' sang Mum,

'Johnny shall have a new master,

He shall have but a penny a day

Because he can't work any faster.'

They ran and jumped and chased each other. They had a turn on the swings.

'Whee . . .' they shouted with each push.

'Up in the sky!' shouted Anthony.

'Look at me!' shouted Mary from the slide.

She was coming down on her tummy like a diver into the water.

'Anybody hungry?' asked Mum. The children didn't answer. They didn't want to go home yet.

'Anybody like a picnic?' said Mum.

'Yes, please!' shouted the children and they all ran to the big picnic table. Out of her bag Mum brought four packets of crisps, two apples, two bananas and an orange.

Mary peeled the orange and divided it into segments.

'Let me count them,' said Anthony and he counted twelve segments.

'Daddy doesn't peel oranges, he cuts them into pieces, doesn't he?' said Mary.

'Why was Daddy shouting?' asked Anthony.

'He was very, very cross,' said Angela, 'and he is not Mummy's friend.'

The children all looked at Mum.

'Yes,' she said, 'he's very, very cross.'

'Is he a baddie?' asked Angela.

'No, darling, when people get cross or hurt or upset they often shout at their families. They don't mean to be nasty, they do it because they're upset.'

'What made Daddy upset?' asked Mary.

'Lots of things, like not having enough money. And because it's not fair.'

'Why isn't it fair, Mum?' asked Mary.

'Well, the people who are in charge won't let everyone have a job, and when you can't get a proper job, you don't have enough money to buy the things you need.'

'Is that why Daddy gets cross?'

'Yes. And then there are the white people who tease him and taunt him and hurt him.'

'Some of them are. Some of them are silly, stupid people who don't stop to think what's really important, like if you're a nice person or good at doing things.'

'My dad's very good at cooking,' said Anthony.

'And dancing,' said Angela.

'And reading stories,' said Mary.

'And making a fire.'

'And mending things.'

'And drilling with his electric drill.'

'And digging the garden.'

Suddenly they heard a little squeaking noise.

'Something is under the table,' said Mary. Carefully the children searched through the long grass.

'Oh!' cried Angela, 'it's a little kitten.'

She picked up the tiny little black kitten. It had silky smooth fur and bright green eyes and it wouldn't stop mewing.

'Can we take her home, please Mum?' she pleaded.

'Yes, I think we'd better. We'll have to try and find out where she's come from. She's so tiny, she should still be with her mother.'

Angela carried the kitten carefully home over the park. Anthony made a bed for her in a cardboard box.

'How can we find the kitten's mother?' he asked.

'I know,' said Mary, 'let's write a notice on a card and put it in the post office window.'

'You clever girl,' said Mum. 'What a good idea.'

So Mary wrote on a card.

```
FOUND!
A very small black kitten with green eyes.
Please phone 41327
```

The woman in the post office took the card to put in the window.

'Well,' she said, 'Mrs Anderson was just telling me her little moggy's had kittens. I wonder if one has strayed. I'll ask her shall I?'

Later, after tea, the phone rang. It was Mrs Anderson. She had lost the kitten, and as she lived in the next street, Mum said they would take her home straight away. Angela started to cry.

'Can't we keep her?' she sobbed.

'Angela, sweetheart,' said Mum, picking her up and holding her close, 'don't cry my precious. Listen to Kitty, now. She's crying and crying, isn't she? She's crying for her own mummy, you know. She wants to go back home.'

'Back home,' repeated Anthony. 'Daddy says 'back home'. He says back home is lovely.'

'Daddy's back home in Jamaica,' said Mary, 'but his home is here.'

'That's right, Mary,' said Mum. 'Back home is the place where he was a baby, then a boy, where he was till he grew up. When you all grow up and live in your own houses, this will be your back home. But now it's just home, for all of us, where we live and love each other.'

Angela climbed off her mum's lap and picked up Kitty.

'Come on,' she said. 'We're taking you back home.'

At Mrs Anderson's house she put the kitten down on the floor. A black and white cat came running over, picked Kitty up in her mouth and carried her back to a big basket where two more kittens were sleeping. She licked Kitty all over and then settled down with all three kittens snuggling up to her.

'She's back home now, isn't she?' said Mary.

Mum and Mrs Anderson looked at each other.

'They'll be needing good homes in three or four weeks' time,' said Mrs Anderson.

'Well children,' said Mum, 'do you think we could offer Kitty a good home when she's old enough to leave her mother?'

'Can we really?' asked Angela.

'Oh! my gladbag is bursting!'

A Hard Lesson

Mary lives with her little sister Angela and little brother Anthony and their mum in a house with a green door near a big park.

All three children like stories. Their favourite stories are about Anansi and Jack the giant killer. They like dinosaurs and Robin Hood stories as well. They ask their mum for a new story about one of their favourites every night.

Mary makes up her own stories too. When she was little her mum used to draw people and animals in cardboard and cut them out for Mary to play with. When she was old enough she made her own cardboard people to play with; they sometimes had very exciting adventures.

Mary's favourite teacher was Mrs Lewis. She had her when she was in Top Juniors. When Mrs Lewis wanted everyone to write a story, Mary always enjoyed doing it. Mrs Lewis liked her stories so much she often read them out to the class.

One day, after she had taken the register, Mrs Lewis told the children to bring their chairs and sit round her desk. They talked about leaving junior school and going to secondary school. Some children were quite worried about it. They thought the big children might tease or bully them. They might find the work too hard. The teachers might not be very nice. They might get a lot of homework. Mary and her friends felt a bit better after talking about their worries with Mrs Lewis. All the children took home letters about changing schools. Some weeks later there were more letters to take home; all the children had got places at the secondary school they wanted.

It was Thursday September 2nd when Mary started at her new school. Luckily, there were quite a lot of boys and girls from her old school in the same class. The school was very big and there seemed to be many teachers. Mary and some of her friends got lost on the way back from science. But their worst fears about older children being nasty to them didn't come true.

Their last lesson was English with Mr Sparks. He asked them what they thought of their new school, if they had been worried before they came, what they felt about it after the first day. Mary thought it was an interesting lesson. She wanted to speak but Mr Sparks never gave her a turn although she kept putting her hand up. Never mind; she would enjoy the homework. Everyone had to write a story called, 'First Day At School'.

Mary wrote about herself, only she used another name. She didn't like her name and wished she had been called Margaret. She gave in her work on Friday morning. Matthew collected all the books and took them to Mr Sparks.

On Monday afternoon they had English again. Mr Sparks walked into the classroom with a big pile of exercise books.

'Well, boys and girls,' he said, 'I'm very pleased with your stories. There were some lovely ideas and excellent writing; I liked your little drawings, too. One or two of you need to work hard at spelling, I think, and I might be asking for extra handwriting practise from you, but on the whole, I'm very pleased. You've made a good start.'

He beamed round the class. Then he glanced at his mark book and his eyes went cold. 'On the other hand,' he said, in a hard voice, staring out of the window, 'there are pupils here who don't seem to understand they are at school to work. We'll come back to that later.'

He gave the books back, making encouraging comments as he did so. When he had only three books left, he stopped. The children were used to this. Mr Sparks was going to read out the best stories.

He read Matthew's first. He made the bit about getting lost on the way back from science sound very funny and everyone laughed. Mr Sparks gave Matthew his book back.

'Now,' said Mr Sparks, holding up Julie's book, 'this is the best piece of work in the whole class.' Mary was puzzled. What was Mr Sparks going to say about her book, then? Mr Sparks read the story and gave back Julie's book. He was silent for several moments, and everyone realised something unusual was about to happen. Mary felt frightened.

Mr Sparks looked at Mary and held up her book. 'Now, boys and girls,' he said, 'this book belongs to our little coloured friend in the second row. Stand up, child; let's look at you. Look at her, boys and girls. Now listen to me. There are two things I will not tolerate - first, no one gives in work late. If I ask for homework on Friday morning, I get it on Friday morning. Is that clear? And the second thing, boys and girls . . .'

Mary's head was spinning. She didn't understand. Mr Sparks was furious, but why? Why was she standing up with everyone looking at her and Mr Sparks in such a terrifying rage?

'And the second thing, boys and girls,' repeated Mr Sparks, 'is *copying*.'

He held up Mary's book, walked up to Mary and sneered, 'If you are so ashamed of your own abilities, my little blackbird, don't think that copying is the answer to your problems. If you're stupid, accept it, work hard, practise your athletics or dancing if you like, but don't hand in work that has been copied out of books. I don't know where you copied it from, I don't want to know, but don't do it again.'

'Please, Mr Sparks,' stammered Mary, 'I didn't copy it, I wrote it, it's my story, ask my friends, they know . . .'

'Get out,' thundered Mr Sparks.

Mary walked out of the classroom. It felt like a savage monster had torn her to pieces. She walked home in a daze and sat down on the step. It seemed ages, but soon afterwards her mum came home from work.

'Darling, my precious, whatever is the matter?'

Sitting there on the step, they clung tightly to each other. When Mary's sobbing quietened, they went inside. She told her mum what had happened.

Mary just wanted to stay on her mother's lap like a baby, being held close until she could fall asleep and escape the terrible nightmare of being awake. But after a little while, her mum made her wash her face and the two of them went back to school. Straight to the headmaster's office they went. Mr Sparks was called. Mary's mum insisted on an apology, but it was very grudging. The headmaster said he was sure it was a misunderstanding, everyone can make mistakes, Mr Sparks was really a very good teacher and he was sure it would not happen again. Mr Sparks said nothing. It was really horrible. As they walked home again, Mary and her mum both agreed that they felt ill.

They collected Angela and Anthony from the childminder's. They had their tea quickly so they could go in the park before bedtime. After Angela and Anthony had gone to bed, Mary and her mum had a long talk.

'Mum,' said Mary, 'I don't want to go to Mr Spark's lessons any more. If I do anything, he'll say it's copied. I can't bear it if he does that again.' But Mary knew she would have to stay in his lessons. 'I won't write good stories, though,' she said, 'I'll scribble some rubbish, the kind of thing he expects from me.'

'No, darling,' said Mum. 'Please don't do that. You must do the very, very best you can. You write such wonderful stories, you mustn't let that stupid, cruel man spoil your chances. You do it in spite of him. You're much much better than he is. Anyway, he won't shout at you again and however nasty he is, the other children will be on your side . . .'

Mary didn't give up. She worked hard and went on writing wonderful stories. Mr Sparks marked them and gave them back to her without a word. He never looked at her if he could avoid it.

A few months later, Mary wrote down the story of what had happened. She wrote it about Margaret and Mr Smart instead of Mary and Mr Sparks. There was a national competition organised by a children's TV programme. Mary sent her story and won the first prize for her age group. The headteacher announced it in assembly and the whole school clapped. He said she was a credit to the school and to her English teacher. But her classmates knew better and so did everyone else when Mary's story was read out on television.

Black Reading Group

The Language Of Love

Words can tell the truth,
But also terrible, loving lies.
To understand what people mean
I have to learn again the language of the eyes,
Hands, shoulders, turn of the cheek,
And to gauge the depth of true love
Know what each little movement implies.

Words can speak the truth.
But it's safer to mark the flow
Of the voice, speaking directly.
Just as I'm sure my pet animals know
From my voice what I'm feeling,
I too could read my mother's tones
Of love, rage or exhaustion long ago.

Words can hide the truth.
Her eyes say her heart will break
For the long suffering man she cherishes.
Her love, rage and exhaustion are all for his sake.
And my cheerful words, week after week
Belie my yearning tones and warm embrace;
I mean, 'Release yourself and her. Please make
An end to this long drawn out desperate heartache.'

As We Are Confident

A long time ago there was a little girl called Patti who lived in Jamaica. Patti lived with her family in a little house with a roof made of coconut-leaf thatch and an earthen floor. There were many little houses just like Patti's close by, and they all belonged to Mr Samuel Sharpe.

Mr Sharpe was a white Englishman. He lived with his family in the Great House, which was so big and so beautiful that it was almost a palace. It had a grand flight of steps up to the magnificent front door. The little houses where Patti and her neighbours lived were well hidden from view of the Great House by a stand of tall breadfruit trees.

Mr Sharpe was very rich. He had an enormous plantation with fields and fields of tall, rustling sugar cane that seemed to go on forever. But Mr Sharpe did not do any work in his fields. Like most rich men, he got other people to do the work for him. Mr Sharp was a backra - a slave-master. Patti's family and all the other families who lived in the little houses behind the breadfruit trees were the ones who did all the hard dangerous work in the canefields. They were the ones who worked to make the sugar which made Mr Sharpe so rich.

Patti could hardly remember a time when she hadn't been tired. She worked hard all day long, looking after the goats, the pigs and the chickens, carrying water, fetching firewood, helping to cook meals for all the other slaves. She was exhausted, aching all over at the end of every day, but still, the evening was the best time. She sat cuddling up with two other girls in a charmed circle of family and friends, held together by the magic of songs and stories. Sometimes they heard tales of Brother Anansi. Then there was an old, old man whose son had joined the Maroons. He was often asked for stories of Cudjoe, Nanny, Johnny Accompong . . .

He described how the redcoat soldiers were sent to flush out the Maroons, how they struggled up the forest paths, sweating and cursing in their smart uniforms, their feet slipping and sliding in their tight leather boots. Everyone held their breath as he told of the Maroon watchman using his abeng to warn the village of the redcoat approach. As swift and silent as shadows, the Maroon soldiers took up their invisible positions round the path. Motionless as treetrunks, perfectly camouflaged with greenery in their hair and clothes, they sprang the perfect ambush. The story made everyone feel good. Knowing that the English had been forced to make a treaty with the Maroons, who still lived free in their own mountain lands, was a great comfort to them all.

Patti listened spellbound to African voices weaving dreams of Africa, visions of slaves flying home to Africa, visions of runaways reaching the safety of Maroon villages, visions of themselves winning freedom for everyone forever.

Some evenings, as Patti sat there, her hair was plaited by Mum or Auntie or Big Sister. when she grew up a bit she would cover her hair with a headtie like all the grown-up women.

Sometimes, instead of songs and stories, the grown-ups talked of their own lives. They shared joys and sorrows, suffering and laughter. The cook from the Great House was a wonderful woman. She was warm, strong, sympathetic and a great healer. She had been born in the stinking hold of a ship in mid-ocean and by a continuing miracle had grown up with her mother who had taught her everything she knew, including her knowledge of herbs and the art of healing. The cook was a wise woman, who knew the power of shared laughter to forge bonds of mutual love and trust, a soothing balm for bruised spirits.

One night, Cook asked everyone what they would do if they worked in the kitchen. She told them to imagine cooking the dinner while the master was sitting in the dining room shouting for his food, 'Bring me my dinner!'

'What do you think I do, then?'

Patti giggled and said, 'You take a little piece of night sage, a teeny little piece and stir it in the pot . . .'

'And then?' asked Cook.

'You swish up the water in your mouth and when it's full you spit it in the pot . . .'

'And then?' asked Cook.

'You carry the pot into the dining room, the master eats it all up and says, oh, it's delicious.'

Cook finished the story . . .

'And then, in the middle of the night, he wakes up with a terrible bellyache. And he moans and groans all night long. And he never knows it's me who made him sick like that . . .'

And they laughed, and laughed and laughed.

But sometimes, the slaves who worked in the Great House had very serious and exciting news to tell. Most inspiring was the name of Toussaint l'Ouverture. If the black people of Haiti could rise up and seize their freedom, if they could defend their hard won liberty against the treachery and aggression of France, Britain and Spain, then surely in Jamaica they too could hope to win freedom in their lifetimes.

As Patti grew up into a young woman, she was sent to work in the canefields every day with the other men and women who were strong and healthy. Naturally, everyone worked as slowly as it was possible to do without being punished. Sometimes, there were little 'problems' or 'accidents' which held up the work and gave everyone a welcome rest. The slaves wore masks of dull passivity while the enraged overseer swore at the carter who was repairing an inexplicably broken trace or examining a limping mule.

Soon after joining the field gang, Patti fell in love. She worked side by side with her young man. At meal breaks, the two of them sat together and their love grew deeper. In the evenings now there were three young couples in the magic circle of story and song, for Patti's two girlhood friends, Juba and Mary, had also fallen in love.

Usually, when a woman is pregnant, it is a wonderful feeling. There is a little baby growing inside her. She thinks, 'My little baby, you will be a bit like me and a bit like your daddy - a miracle of love between us . . . Who will you be . . . ? Are you a boy or a girl . . . ? I don't know, it doesn't matter. Oh! Feel the baby move! Was it a kick or a punch? This little one will be a fighter, anyway.'

And when the baby is born, she holds her little one close and murmurs, 'You're the very baby I've always wanted.'

But Patti could not feel joyful like that. Her baby was going to be a slave. Her child would belong to Mr Sharpe. Anything could happen. Mr Sharpe could even take her baby to sell, and she would never see her little one again. Or, if the child did grow up with her, how could she bear to see her own child whipped or tortured? The brutal fact of belonging to another person was intolerable.

44   Black Reading Group

Patti talked about her feelings with Juba and Mary. Juba was overwhelmed with grief, bitterness and anger. She was determined that Mr Sharpe should never own her child. She asked their wise friend the cook for help. Cook listened gravely. She put her arms round Juba, put her ear to her belly and listened to the baby inside. Then she gave Juba a tiny bottle of poison she had prepared from roots and leaves.

Juba wept as she swallowed the bitter draught. It did not kill her but it killed the baby inside her. Soon afterwards her baby was born, a beautiful little girl - but she was dead. Juba held her little dead baby and wept in anguish. They wrapped the little one gently in a clean cloth and buried her in grief, bitterness and anger.

Mary did not want to take poison, but, like Juba, she could not bear her child to be a slave. Her baby was born alive and well, a beautiful little boy. Mary held her baby close, very close. With infinite love and tenderness she pressed his little mouth and nose to her breast. He could not breathe and in a few seconds he was dead. They wrapped the little one gently in a clean cloth and buried him too in grief, bitterness and anger.

When Patti's time came, her baby was born alive and well, a beautiful little boy. Patti held him and looked in his eyes. She did not want him to be a slave, but she could not bear to kill him. She loved the baby's father and believed their son would have the same courage, strength and intelligence. Her mind was full of stories she had heard from childhood of Cudjoe and Toussaint. She had a strong faith that her child would be as great a man as they. So she cradled her baby in her arms, and sang to him in a low sweet voice.

Mr Sharpe came to see the new slave boy. Patti had to watch while he picked up her child, looked at him and said, 'Hm, this one is good-looking, isn't he? Give him my name - Samuel Sharpe.'

Patti was angry but she bit her lip and said nothing. Why couldn't *she* choose the baby's name? Why couldn't she call him after his father, or after Cudjoe? Well, even if she couldn't choose the name, she made sure to follow the customs of her people. The navel string was buried and a mango seed planted. This would always be her child's own tree. Patti also made sure his hair was not cut - at least until he could speak properly.

Little Sam was a beautiful child. Soon he could sit up, then stand up, holding onto his mother. When he was one he could walk, when he was two he knew a lot of words, when he was three he could talk very well, just like most children. He was very curious, he was always asking everybody questions and he listened carefully to what people said. So he learnt a lot and grew up to be very intelligent.

Sam had to work hard like everyone else, but he was not cruelly or brutally treated. He did not go to school. Slaves did not go to school, but Sam managed to learn to read. Most of all he liked reading the Bible - that's the Holy Book with stories of Moses, Daniel, David and Jesus. He read all those stories. He read that God knows and loves every single person, that all are equal in His sight and that none has the right to hold another in bondage.

From being a good listener and an avid reader, Sam became a marvellous speaker. The power of his words was so irresistible that he could move his listeners to tears of anguish or of joy, cries of exultation or of anger. When he was a grown-up man his owner and the church minister allowed him to speak to religious gatherings of slaves on all the plantations round about. Do you think he spoke only of religion? Of course not! He spoke of the intolerable evil of slavery, asserting it was against the will of God and the teaching of Jesus. Sam noticed those people who were set alight by his preaching and talked with them for hours after the others had all gone to bed.

Gradually a plan formed in his head, a plan that was brilliant, courageous and totally dependent on the loyalty and secrecy of his friends. Now, if you were a slave and you knew of a plan to escape or to fight, the pressure to tell the master was enormous. If you were found out, they would torture you with horrible cruelty and those who loved you would be forced to watch your death. They might even be tortured as well. Yet in spite of this pressure, Sam inspired such loyalty in his listeners that no one gave away the secret plan, no one told. Sam's unshakeable belief in the right to live in freedom, in the duty to fight for freedom and in the possibility of winning freedom, was so powerfully communicated that 20,000 slaves joined the rebellion that he had planned with all his skill, intelligence and commitment.

This was the plan . . . at Christmas time, the slaves always had 3 days off work, 3 days for family and friends, 3 days for drumming and dancing, for music and masquerade, for songs and stories. But this Christmas, they had 3 days to prepare for Sam's plan. On the last evening of the holiday, the slaves were supposed to go to the overseer as usual to be told what their work was next day. But this year was different. 20,000 slaves simply said they would only work if they were paid proper wages.

The overseers were stunned. They could not believe it. The plantation owners were shocked. The action was so widespread they could not imagine how it could have been so successfully organised. When they refused to listen to the demand and called out the soldiers to force the slaves back to work, then violence and destruction erupted. Much blood was shed and more than a million pounds worth of damage was done before the rebellion was crushed.

Yes, they did catch Sam and his friends. In the prison, Sam told a minister who came to visit him, 'I would rather die upon yonder gallows than live in slavery.'

They hanged him on May 23rd 1832.

But the rebellion Sam had so brilliantly organised terrified the plantation owners. They realised the slaves were ready to seize their freedom whatever the cost in blood and sacrifice. And so, the very next year after Sam's death, the Parliament in London made a new law to say that there should be an end to slavery.

What do you think Sam's mother felt then? Very sad that Sam was dead? Yes, she would cry. Yes, she would miss him terribly. But she would be proud of him. She would be glad that her son had helped bring an end to slavery.

Is that the end of the story? No. The story hasn't finished yet. We are part of the story ourselves. The story of resistance will finish when

. . . well, let's listen to Bob Marley sing the end of the story . . .

'Until the philosophy that holds one race superior and another inferior is finally and totally discredited and abandoned, everywhere is war, war . . .

. . . We Africans will fight, we find it necessary. And we know we shall win, as we are confident in the victory of good over evil . . .'

Carl Green receiving the Sister Dora award from Noddy Holder on behalf of the Black Reading Group.

Carl Green

Carl Green is from Jamaica and is influenced by travelling and is very educational. There is always something new to learn when meeting people. He finds that everyone has different influences and a different view to things. This has given him another way of keeping an open mind about things and people.

He is active in the community in many ways such as working voluntarily with community organisations doing counselling and is presently completing training in Community Mediation with the Wolverhampton Mediation Services. He also works voluntarily with the Black Reading Group.

He was fortunate to act a part in a short film. He has done a bit of script writing for short films and also works as a camera man behind the scenes. He writes poetry to allow him to express some of his views of how he sees things and thinks of them. He said: 'If I am to leave anything to myself, then I see poetry as something good in all respects.'

It Is So True

'I was with nature, before I was given on to my father.
             For how long.'
             Don't ask me.
             Ask Mother
             Nature, she
              Knows!

I was within my father before I was given to my mother, yes!
I was chosen by nature then, 'And yes it is so.
             For how long.'
             Don't ask me.
             Ask Mother

             Nature, she

'O, yes I sure did spend some time within my mother in
a world well protected by her and Mother Nature, who has not
deserted me from that moment I was created, to this minuet.'

             For how long I was with my father,
             I don't know?
             For how long I was within my mother,
             Before I was born, it could be from one
             To nine months, I do now!

O

O, Mother, O, Father I am hooked on the substance that
you took in you before I was born, I get it from you straight
in my blood stream before I was born, and now, I am hooked
it brings about an appetite that has no depth, it brings about
a constant crave for more and more of the Whites, the Brown
the use of the needle, and other things that I just don't know
the names, I have been to the doctor and he
try to help me with the little he have
and he told me he is now
running out of
stock and
I can't go
back.

O, Mother, O, Father I am hooked on the substance you took long before
I was born I got it from you straight out of your blood stream and now It
is affecting me, it brings about this constant thirst that have no limes
I Am always in this constant need for more of this thing that is called
the Brown, White, the need for the use of the needle. O I am trapped,
trapped in this body of mine wanting to rid myself of it all. This blood
stream, the thirst, the crave, the strain, the pain that it brings to my
brain, that is driving me insane O.
The doctor told me that his stock
Is running out and he can't tell me
Tell me when he will get more
He don't know
When
His
Next
Supply
Will
Arrive
O,
Mother,
O,
Father,
I
hooked

from
the
substances
taken in by
either of
you!

O,
O.
I am so, so hooked my
dear Mother and Father!

Pauline Janke

Pauline Janke was born in Birmingham of Jamaican parentage. She has been a secondary school teacher since 1993 and has been writing since the age of 13. She is married with a 6-year-old son and has lived in Germany and the USA. She speaks German.

Pauline is currently finishing her Master of Education degree in special education and inclusion at Birmingham University.

The Negress

(Inspired by The Negress, 1880; a painting by Marie-Guillermine Benoist)

Did they perceive the beauty which embodied you?
Circling the rounds of your heels
And extending to the curves of your hips
Which swayed easily to the rhythm of distant drums
Vibrating.
Did they behold the warm glow of your gloss brown eyes?
Like marbles, which glimpsed all, and gathered all
Which gazed diligently as the earth drained dry
Like your sleeping eyes
With no more tears to fall.
What did they hear from your lips?
Soft and coloured like the earth
Sweet like the juice of the naseberry, that they tasted
When they fell upon you,
Girding you like the linen wrapped about your muscular loins
Making your basket full with fruit for a season.
And as the cloak of passion held you, grappling silky soft hide
Shadowing like velvet,
Did they feel the burning in your breast?
Like pride desiring to erupt like volcanoes.
Softly simmering in the steam of his night
Sleep cradles you into morning,
And your carcass sits still,
As if with lips wrapped firmly around the truth of your existence
Eyes still whispering
Do you see me?

Miesha Johnson

Miesha Johnson is 14 years old and is a new writer. She has been writing short stories and poems since she was 6 or 7 years old. Miesha has entered competitions at local libraries and she said one of her poems was published by a firm looking for young writers.

Miesha said that her inspiration for the poems that she writes comes from everyday experiences, thoughts or incidents that happen which make her want to write. She enjoys reading and the arts especially performing arts.

Urban Safety

The street's
A place to meet
To greet
To say hi
To say bye
To have fun
In the sun
Or in the rain
It doesn't matter
Friends in the urban society

The street's
A place of madness
Of sadness
Of wounding
Of bleeding
Of screaming
Of confusion
Of illusion
When hiding or waiting
It doesn't matter
Enemies in the urban society

The street's
A place where so many give in
The delusion of the profusion
Of having too much of a bad thing
Substances you can't reject
That reflects your persona
When you're with so-called friends
It doesn't matter
Be careful who you're friends with in the urban society

Mothers

Mothers are confusing creatures
Can be ugly but have your features
Why is she so mad?
I don't know
Must be something stupid though

When you argue take it from me
Moms can have the force of three
But then they twitch
Like flicking a switch
The dark side's gone and now the light
Suddenly you're allowed to be right!

As long as you're who you're told to be
You won't see this side during PMT
But lucky because these times are few
You can lie, cry, sing as you do

Still it's hard to understand them though
First you're free and then on death row
Do they understand me at all?
I just know it's bad if I hear my name call

Mother dear please explain!
How you're both nice and a pain.

Norma Jean Johnson

Norma Jean Johnson is known as Talibah to close friends and the performing world. She says that Talibah means seeking after knowledge. She is a singer and songwriter and started doing this at the age of 14. She plays a guitar and is also learning to play the keyboard and read music.

Talibah has been writing poetry for a year on and off and she says that she enjoys it as it helps to eliminate stress giving her a different focus on life.

Respect

I am not sorry I am a woman
I am not sorry I am black
I'm just sorry I cannot turn the clock back
I was so immature not knowing what to do
Looking for, not checking you and me out
Making sure.
Mama said get a rich man, I didn't mine
Poor, and when my friends rejected me
Papa said one friend will be enough.

Sure I convince myself everything would
Be AOK as I climb into my safety pocket
Zone not too far to roam, was I so desperate?
Naa - but I struggled, tossing and turning on
The Issues residing in my mind.

How do you want to know me, is this love
On the line?

Your slaver mentality tries to consume me,
Confusing me with superstition and rituals
Passed down from the slave master
Misinterpreting dissecting me from what I am
And what I am supposed to transcend into
As a human being.

Do you respect me? Do I hold your interest?
Do you wish to know my views? Or is it, I must
Play the fool ignorant, just to keep you amused,
Like an empty cup you want to fill me up.
Do you not see the need to accept the seed that has been
Planted in me? The seed that has grown into a tree,
I am that, I am and all I need to be.

Your lustful desire dethrones me and lets me look less
Than how I should be! Never you forget this, you can't
Stop me. See my talent flexing as I break free to fulfil
The gifts in me I pray tell me you can respect my interest
Have you no need to be blessed with the sugars of my conquest.

I am the universe, the planets are my seeds
And each seed that is discovered is so unique.
Time will set me free, and from this freedom
I will fulfil the role I was born for. You see no more
Am I so immature, I have grown and still growing can
You respect the needs in me, do I hold your interest if
Not, then let me be so some other dude may invest.

The time is near.

Dam Fast And Cravin

Dam fast and cravin
Me should a shut me mouth
Overnight food dis a cut me belly out,
Fever start fe teck me as the food me belly
It a operate,
It did have a slight whiff, but me never hesitate.
Me nam it same way, and clean off the plate.

Wooy the pain dis a bite it feel like
Tonight a me last night.

Lard spear me from submitting to appetite,
Me da push so till me tripe soon come out
Dis wouldn't a happen if me just shut me mouth.

Wooy fast and cravin it never work out
Lard a god phone the ambulance car me
Dis-a go past out.

The food tuck in a me gut a turn primordial
Soup, stinkier than the dead carcass them
Wa-dea-a bay-root.
Me dea- rub me belly me dea - tell you
The truth, Duppy dea - laugh a sah you
Brute, the next time you give in to appetite
Dam Fast and Cravin a go meck you have
Sleepless night.

Somewhere in the Walsall borough.

Black Reading Group

Francis Page

Francis Page is 41 years old and lives in Walsall, in the West Midlands, and is a member of the Black Reading Group.

When he was 6 or 7 years old, he played the part of a broomstick, in the 'Sorcerer's Apprentice' at Walsall Town Hall. When he was 9 or 10 years of age he achieved a certificate for swimming. He joined the RAF cadets at 14 years old and got a first-class badge, with a badge for target practice with a 303 rifle.

He has also had a poem published in a magazine with other poems published in books. He has performed his poetry at Walsall Town Hall, Pleck Library and Caldmore Green Club. Francis also enjoys writing and performing poetry. He said that for him, it is a passion.

A Rhythmic Lines Production

The Story Of Mo Maisey

Written and produced

by

Francis Page

The Story Of Mo Maisy

In New York City, around the time of nineteen-thirty, there lived a night-club jazz singer, by the name of Mo Maisey. And Mo to most people was considered a daisy.

On stage, she'd sing and dance. Off, she'd practise hard and her act, she would enhance.

Black African American she was, but in colour, very light. And with a voice like velvet, she would sing softly through the night.

In nineteen-hundred and three, she was born, and for a living her parents grew and cut corn. And Mo originally came from Illinois, her father threw her out after she became friendly with a white farm boy.

She came to Harlem to live with her aunt, in her youth. And of her background, to people she never disclosed the truth.

She discovered her talent as a singer, whilst at church, as a chorister and bell-ringer. And now Mo, a Christian, and almost twenty-seven, she had no doubts in the slightest about going to Heaven.

And there was a man in Mo's life, a doorman named Spats Loint, who had worked the doors of every small-time Harlem joint. They called him Spats as he had a passion for shoes, and Spats played a little trumpet, and sang a little blues.

And Mo and Spats lived in a downtown tenement block, with having no time to lounge around, as they lived around the clock.

The two hardly earned enough dollars for rent, food, bills, etcetera, even for Mo's stunning stage dresses, they worked hard for the extra.

And Mo loved Spats with all of her heart, and in both their eyes, the two could never be apart. Even close friends could tell there were to be rings of a wedding bell.

And then one night at the club, after Mo was to dance and sing, Spats gave Mo flowers, with a proposal, and when Mo accepted, the two were in elation, spending the rest of the evening in celebration.

The marriage ceremony was grand, they even hired a piano player to play upon a stand. And the cake was three-tier, and the guests were in a happy mood of cheer.

Though now, several months later, and now man and wife, it was time for Mo and Spats to get on with their life.

One evening the night-club had a very special visitor, and the revellers could not believe their eyes, as everywhere around the club there were gasps and sighs.

It was none other than Earl Heinze; one of the greatest musicians of these jazz times. And after he saw Mo doing her performance, which Heinze thought a steal, he offered Mo a lucrative deal.

And with news so great, Mo phoned her aunt, to tell her of her fate. It was for Mo, to be the bright lights of Broadway, and this Mo Maisey never thought she would live to see the day.

And very soon, within the Broadway sights, the name 'Mo Maisey' went up in lights. And with her name, the papers told of her success and fame.

And with a growing fortune, Mo bought a five-bedroom house, in Manhattan, and she and Spats picnicked for Sunday fun in Staten.

And now with Spats as Mo's minder, the times they had together could not have been finer. And Mo went on tour, singing alongside the likes of Armstrong, and all the greats, in almost every city of the American states.

Though several years later, Spats began to feel the stress, as every evening before Mo's performance, she would slip into another elegant dress.

Spats became resentful to Mo through her attention to other guys, as they swarmed around Mo like flies. Spats began to feel a dying light, and for relaxation, go from bar to bar, and visit the odd lady of the night.

Spats by now had become to live a double life, with no regard for morals or his wife. Though Mo began to pick-up on Spat's drinking, Mo's mind came to thinking. She put Spats on a sort of trial, but Spats as he was, was in denial.

And with Spat's condition, Mo's nerves were put to the test, as Mo for Spats did her very best. She even tried to admit Spats to a clinic, but to no use, as Spats was by now a far-gone alcoholic.

And as Mo carried on with her career, she could only watch as the man she dearly loved would drown himself in spirits and beer. Even her fame and fortune could not save them from this, how could their lives be so far from bliss?

And on the stage, the pretence was too much for Mo as after, in the dressing room, into a fit of tears she would go.

It was now nineteen-forty-five, and Mo's singing career began to take a dive. A new era brought new music, swing and jive. At the box office, Mo's name was not selling, and for Spats in his body and face, his time was telling.

Spats by now was housebound, due to his failing liver, and for the sight of the housemaids, he made them shiver. Though he still had a nip of gin from the many bottles he had specially brought in.

One evening, after Mo sang at Carnegie Hall, she was to receive a very distressing call. She rushed home to find a doctor beside Spat's bed, but for Mo's concern it was too late, as Spats was dead.

Mo was in grief though Spat's dying, as at the funeral friends and colleagues were crying. Though for six more years, Mo continued with the stage and sang, whilst in her head, the memory of Spats and his voice rang.

And in nineteen fifty-one, Mo Maisey retired leaving many a young jazz musician inspired. She never remarried and became a recluse, living in Spain, having her servants play her records over and over again.

Mo Maisey lived for another thirty-one years, with her fondest memories that brought her tears. And in nineteen-eighty-five, at the age of eighty-two, Mo Maisey died from pneumonia and the flu.

When The Candle Dies

In the dark the candle burns slowly,
I read the Father's book and feel a spirit so holy.
And after the candle dies, in my dreams the Devil tells lies.

There's an almighty battle in the skies,
there's thunder and lightning,
and the dream becomes frightening.

And in the light when I awake,
the Devil has been banished
through God's sake.

God's Will

Perhaps it was God's will, that made me ill.
Drinking too much and taking pills.

My mind like a camera flashing,
taking stills.

The Old Man

See the old man there,
a hero who won medals fighting in the war,
now he looks through the rubbish bins and picks cigarette ends up
off the floor.

And because no one cares and no one wants to hold the blame
he sleeps in the streets at night in the cold, the wind, and the rain.
He has a daughter that lives not too far away
but she does not care for him and says he is not her father anyway,

he tries to stand in the warm foyer of the library
but the staff there throw him out because he is so scruffy and untidy.
And as the council officials walk by the stop and buy store,
for £1 he asks them, but he is ignored,

so he continues to sleep in the streets at night in the cold,
the wind and the rain, because no one cares and no one wants
to hold the blame.

And sometimes if you look closely you can see tears in his eyes
perhaps he is thinking of his wife and the day she died,
she took a shopping trip into town
and while crossing the busy road she got knocked down
the driver of the car was never found.

So now he wanders around the town in a confused state of mind
him and many old folks of his kind.
And tonight he will continue to sleep in the streets in the cold,
wind and rain, because no one cares and no one wants
to hold the blame.

The Family

The family washing hangs upon the line to dry,
and the husband's white shirt collars still show dirt and grime.
And upon the four foot door that acts as a garden gate,
'Beware Of The Dog' is written in black and green paint.

Visitors now take a different route,
unbeknown, their dog is over their neighbour's garden
fertilising the beetroot shoots.
And high upon a shelf in their woodworm-riddled shed,
tadpoles swim in rusty baked bean tins,
their youngest son has an interest in such botanical things.

And the husband's DIY - a job done fine
with polythene covering the kitchen window
that's been broken seven times.
And their teenage daughter sits in her bedroom alone,
there she dreams of pop stars and boys as she watches
the 45's spin around.

Their grandfather, 74 and frail, slips on the foot of the stairs
spilling the contents of his night pail.
And their mother oblivious to the noise from him,
she plays radio's lucky bingo in the kitchen,
though she's never won a thing.
And upon the well-worn carpet in their living room
stands a black PVC settee upon which lies their jobless son
watching the racing on TV.

And a family of brass geese hang proudly from their wall,
a present from their grandmother from a *Blackpool* seafront stall.
And in a glass vase on the window sill, the dry red roses have died
of their own free will.

And when a certain neighbour calls round, the *family* are never in
and there's never a sound, all through an argument over fifteen pounds
that the neighbour claims the *family* owes.
And on Sunday's their relatives call around for tea,
corned beef sandwiches and pickles they eat with chocolate cake
and mugs of tea, all twelve members of the *family.*

Caribbean Dreams

Soup, bun and cheese, I'd like to sit under a Caribbean sun in ease. Curried goat, rice and peas, I'd like to feel the Caribbean breeze running through the trees.

Cassava and plantain, I'd like to climb the highest Caribbean mountain. Jerk chicken in a leaf woven dish, I'd like to swim in a Caribbean sea with the flying fish.

Dumplings and bulla, I'd like to meet a Caribbean girl named Hula. Sweet potatoes and yam, I'd like to walk upon a Caribbean beach with her, it would be so glam.

Fresh tomatoes, lettuce, sardines, we all have 'Caribbean Dreams'.

Stand Tall

Stand tall black man and walk through God's light and shine,
like Bruno, Lewis and Ali. You're all God's children so fine.

You are strong, beautiful, unique. Stand tall when the racists speak.
Find yourselves like Haley, and do your best.

But don't walk extremely as Mr X.

Like the Reverend King, make yourselves heard to the people of all.
Like Areatha and Ella, sing in your strongest voice in the Gospel Hall.

For there will come a day when good will come your way.

Love yourselves, love your brothers and sisters across the ocean too
and love them all.

And remember black man, stand tall.

A V-Bomb Fell

A V-bomb fell in Cardale Street
it missed Mrs Lewis by twenty-eight feet.
Poor Mrs Lewis, angry and shocked
cursed those German pilots with her kitchen mop.

Such was the noise that the neighbours came out
and calmed Mrs Lewis with two bottles of stout.
She cried about her loved one Bert, who'd gone away to sea,
his ship hit by a U-boat and now a prisoner in Germany.

A V-bomb fell in Cardale Street
it hit our local butcher shop and now we've got no meat.
The owner Mr Willis got his Enfield gun
fired two shots in the air but didn't kill no one.

The Home Guards came and calmed him down
and sat him in a chair, he cried about a loved one.
His only living son who'd marched away to Europe
to face those German guns.

A V-bomb fell in Cardle Street
it fell on Charlie Gibson's bakery.
The neighbours stood their worried
and the firemen searched in vain.
Old Mr Gibson staggered up the street drunk
singing, *'We'll Meet Again'*.

With tears in his eyes and strong morale
he sang the last few words of his song.
Then he cried about his loved one, Monique,
whom he met during his time on the Somme.

A V-bomb fell in Cardle Street
it hit our house at number thirty-three.
My father, my mom, my sister and me
haven't got a home and become refuges.

They put me on a large ship that sailed to a cold country,
I've cried about my loved ones, I really miss my family.
So now I'll send my love from Quebec,
to the people of Cardale Street.

Baggshaw's Days

In Pastor Baggshaw's preaching days, of God he spoke, urging people
to change their ways.
Large crowds he drew at functions and fairs, as the folk walked by,
they would stop to listen and stare,
at his eyes that glared, whilst he bared the truth of the good
Lord's words.
'Give your soul to God, throw away your sinful ways.

Etc, etc!' he'd say, whilst he read the quotes from biblical days.
All England he toured, in all weathers endured,
he preached from horseback from Cornwall to Hull.

Yet these were the usual teachings of the day and a popular guest
at dinners be became,
in the houses and mansions of dignitaries he stayed, for these were
Baggshaw's glorious day.

From the young and old; he captured souls, from the sermons
and speeches he read on his troth, and a place in Heaven he promised
those souls, in return they would build him a church.
Their silver, their gold, their wares they sold and lined the pockets of
Baggshaw's clothes.
For this church, they gave and gave, while the deceptive
Pastor stashed it away.

A payment for the timber and stone was due to be made, but money
in the bank, 'There is none!' the clerk explained, 'nor had there ever
been any investment made,' he repeated again.
And though this was the day for the work to begin, Pastor Baggshaw
was nowhere to be seen.
Through the dark and narrow streets they searched, with torches of fire,
across fields and downs, until the folk tired.

For now they had come to realise the Pastor was a swindler and liar,
and of this a sheriff was notified and hired; the reward, a bag of gold
coins, more than the wealthiest of men could earn in five years and of
the Pastor's treachery, the people began to hear.

Almost eight months and one week had passed since that ill-fated day,
and Baggshaw was considered as wealthy, and far away.

But in a southern English coastal town, a Mr J Brady arrived at an inn and for the night he stayed, with the intention of boarding a ship in the early morning light, to sail to the French port of Calais.

That following morning at the breakfast table at the inn, Mr Brady noticed a peculiar thing. For across the room a Pastor sat with luggage beside him.

Mr Brady then left that inn and at the dockside informed a passing soldier about who he had seen. But as the soldier looked into Mr Brady's eyes, he very soon realised. For he was staring into the eyes]of the man whose eyes glared, as he bared the truth of the good Lord's words, for this was Baggshaw.

He was seized and taken back to that town, where during his trial, hundreds of people gathered around, and guilty of theft and treachery to be found.

And in the year of their Lord in 1783, Baggshaw was hanged and left to lie in an unmarked grave in a Northern cemetery.
'It seems the good Lord's words were spoken indeed.'

Clifton Pinnock

My name is Clifton. I have been writing poetry for about twenty years. I regard my poetry as a very enjoyable hobby. I take pleasure in all types of poetry, especially humorous ones, though I do not write them myself.

I write on various themes though I mostly write about the natural beauty about me, therefore I think of myself as a nature poet. I am a Christian and a family man with a beautiful and caring wife and three grown-up children, all of whom support me in my poetry.

I see myself as an African, born and raised in Jamaica and now residing in England. My desire is to build up myself, my people and community spiritually, as well as socially. This I believe can be achieved through education, ie teaching from the Bible and learning of the achievements and contributions of Africans from earliest times. This will enlighten both Africans and non-Africans and would empower Africans to build our self-image, self pride and self-esteem. My poetry can also be a contributory factor.

I have performed at various places over the West Midlands, eg Walsall, Sandwell and Birmingham. I have had my poems published from a number of sources, eg newspapers, books and journals. I have also been featured in the newspapers - The Express and Star and the Birmingham Evening Mail.

My desire is that folk will enjoy my poetry and it will be a source of inspiration for all.

African Girl

She holds her head high:
Her chin protrudes gracefully;
As she strolls by
Her rugged African hillside.

Her motley array of beads
Cascade down:
Her swan-like ebony neck;
Looking exotic and delightful.

Her tall willowy figure;
Mesmerises me,
As she moves coolly and wavely along;
Swaying gently,
As she strides by the scabious throng.

Her visage with an admirable smile:
Elegant, comely and kind;
Warms me:
Infusing me with joy,
Tempting me to reach out and touch her golden face.
Such a face, cool, black, beautiful face.

She continues on her way,
With her multicoloured garments
Elegantly complimenting her swarthy skin;
And cladding flimsily to her
As if they are destined to fall off
To expose fully, her skin;
Such skin, gorgeous radiant black skin;

Beauty so fine,
Colour sublime;
Lady of mine,
Stay as you are, dark and lovely.
An appreciation of women
And a delight to men.

She disappears now into the tunnel of the horizon.
Only a memory of her is left:
A souvenir of a resplendent pearl;
But! What a memory!
My African girl.

Be Proud To Be An African

If you have some African blood in you
You are an African.

Whether you have a little or a lot
It doesn't matter how much you've got
You are an African.

Like every race
We have our faults and our failures
Our victories and our grace.

So wherever you were born
And whatever shade you are
Be proud of your heritage
Be proud to be an African.

I Remember Jamaica

I remember Jamaica
Land of fun and beauty
Packed with charm and adventure.

I remember Jamaica
With its tall breadfruit plants
And their mighty fruit swaying gently in the driving breeze.

I remember the blue tits and Johnny birds,
Eating the lovely sweetsop
We took out our catapults and made a shot.

I remember the dogwood trees,
As lads we climbed to the top centre branch
And then heaved up and down in the propelling breeze.

I remember the hills we trudged
To reach their plateaued summit
Then sat down and viewed with thrill, the exhilarating scenes.

I remember the cricket we played,
Satiating ourselves with the fun of the game, anytime of the day.

I remember the fire lanterns at night
How their twinkling lights pierced the dark
Shining through the woods, looking like sparkling stars.

I remember blissful school days
Play was so pleasant
There was football, baseball and 'hide and seek' amongst the sisal plants.

I remember the fast flowing rivers,
We would swim and fish
Then take the catch home and have a delectable dish.

I remember the deep blue sea,
Children dipping and diving
Whilst on the pure white sands, others eating and relaxing.

Oh yes, I remember Jamaica!
Land of fun and beauty
Land given to us by a kind Creator.

Black Reading Group

I See God

I see God through nature;
I see His tenderness in many a creature.

I see His beauty in the flowers;
And in birds of varied colours.

Through the family I see His kindness;
Causing man, woman and child to reap happiness.

I see His power in holding up the planets;
And even providing protection for the stinging hornets.

I see His dexterity in forming the body;
Excellent, intricate and of great beauty.

I see His thoughtfulness in giving us delicious foods;
And other precious life-sustaining goods.

I see His care in preserving us from evil;
And rescuing us from many a peril.

I see His love in giving us advice;
Praise be to Him for wanting us to be with Him in paradise.

Loving

Loving is saying words that are pleasant
And offering smiles that are kind and elegant.

Loving is, after a day away from home
You greet your partner with a hug and kiss.

Loving is bringing her home a bouquet of flowers
Showing her how beautiful her affection is to you.

Loving is giving her your very last
Though it be your absolute favourite.

Loving is telling your partner
'I love you.'

Loving is saying, 'I am sorry'
When you have hurt someone.

Loving is looking, not on the colour or the class
But treating him or her as a friend.

If practised, the motion of loving;
Then life can really be rewarding.

Away from loving, please do not run
For loving can be such fun.

There Is A Lot Of Beauty In Them:
Folk With Disabilities

There is a lot of beauty in them: those folk with disabilities
And we could see it;
If only we would take a closer look.

What with all that wincing and winding!
And the seeming agonising strain as they speak
Along with their mangled hands and disfigured feet.
Can you really say that there is beauty in them?

Yes if only we would take a closer look! We could see it,
Just like the newly-formed butterfly;
Fighting to get out of its disguising husks;
The beauty of the disabled is fighting its way out:
Away from its concealing shucks.

Oh, wrench open the shell; let the beauty out!
Capture it, hold it, admire it.

Life is not measured by how fast one can run;
Nor how many trophies in a season, you have won.
Or even how many thousands of pounds accumulated;
It is the giving of love that is counted.

Look at their eyes, what do you see?
I see a sparkle!
Their eyes of love are beckoning;
Calling out to share their affection.

If they have no eyes, they have hands; hands ready to embrace.
If they have no hands, they have mouths; mouths ready to thank you.

Please look!
Look at them essentially;
Do not look at their disability.
If they have no feet, nor hands, nor eyes, nor ears, nor mouth,
Still look!

Look at them, love them;
When you see each for what he or she is: a human,
You will love them.
You will not ponder on expense; you will just care.

Love them;
What do you want in return?
I ask, 'What is the greatest gift?
Is it not love?'
They will give their greatest gift.
Please give them yours.

There is a lot of beauty in them: folk with disabilities,
And we could see it,
If only we would take a closer look.

My Wife

My wife, she blossoms like a rose in the morning
The royal ponsietta tree
When in full bloom, with its elegant red flowers,
Cannot compare with her.

When the curtains I pull back at morn
And the luminary orb shines on her exquisite dark face
Even a budding apple tree, full of pink and white florets,
Glistening radiantly in the bright sunlight
Would pale into insignificance in her presence.

My wife, she does me good, never harm:
I put my confidence in her and I will never be poor.

She is a hard worker, strong and industrious.
She is generous,
She always looks after her family's needs:
Her children appreciate her
And I praise her:
    Many women are good wives,
    But you are the best of them all.

    He who findeth a wife has done well,
    For she is worth far more than jewels,
    It shows that Jehovah is good to you.

What a lucky chap I am,
Aye!
My wife, she does blossom like a rose in the morning.

A Ramble In Walsall

Tired of sitting down,
The thought of a little walk in my mind was sown,
Walking, loiteringly along the road;
I stopped to watch the carefree juvenile crowd.

Unsatisfied like a grazing horse,
I casually continued on my course.
Towards the bridging wooden planks
Glancing around as I go on, the rubbishy clovered banks.

On reaching the bridge I paused to muse;
Looking down below where the much clearer waters used to cruise.
Oh what a pity, now only a small stream flows on one side;
Trickling gently down to the gully where the green trees bide.

I watched some children play on the swampy bed,
As well as others in their gardens, far ahead.
But as I look around on the green fields below;
Something began to pull me, yes, I must go!

In front of me the landscape was so shapefully spanned;
Scrutinising you would think, it was designed by hand.
I take my stroll, oh so carefreely down the efflorescenced hill;
Infusing with beauty my eyes as I stopped by, for them to fill.

I carried on walking on my carpet of green,
Listening transportingly to the little birds as they tunefully scream.
But what is this other soothing tone I hear?
It is indeed a lovely unfamiliar sound, attracting my ear.

My curiosity got the better of me,
And I plunged through the twiggy fence to see,
There it was, the balm that was drawing
Those feet of mine to give my mind some calming.

I stood by the stream for nearly an hour,
Passionately absorbing the pleasantries of nature's healing power.
On my mind it had some marvellous effects,
That wending, crawling stream, as down its course it ejects.

Black Reading Group

It was a haven there;
For nature had banished my care.
She used the stereophonic sounds of the waters lapping on each ledge;
And the melody of the dazzling birds as they spring
from hedge to hedge.

My pleasure was only marred
By some empty cans, the crappie clothes that slimly scared
My miniature river bed,
And my nearby pastel meadow-spread.

Nevertheless, I walked away from my bliss;
Feeling contented; by knowing this.
That although my scenery was slightly afflict'd
I did enjoy my Maker's gift.

I sauntered back to church, over the dandelioned and primrosed
field of grass;
Determined to keep in my head the experience I had just passed;
I sat in my pew, thanked my Creator and hoped that we will take care
Of this wonderful world that we share.

Somewhere in the Walsall borough.

Black Reading Group

Jacqueline Elizabeth Taylor

Jacqueline Elizabeth Taylor has always had a passion for words as far back as she can remember. At 4 years old she found immense pleasure learning to spell words, rhyme and articulate them to an audience; namely her parents, teachers and whoever would indulge. She also enjoys reading and it is still a passion to this day!

Her inspiration for her work comes from life experiences, observation of people, nature and at times from a source outside herself.

She has a dream to write a book that would empower others to believe that they can achieve, with the unique gifts that each one of us possesses, regardless of the circumstances, or setbacks. She says that each one of us has the innate power to create our own script!

Saturday Night

'I'm gonna kill you,' growling viciously - his hands fastened tightly around my neck like a vice. My heart pounded against the cage of my ribs, fear filled my being. I prayed silently for deliverance. Suddenly! I'm released from his deathly grip. My eyes fly open and I realise that it's just a dream. Thank God he's gone now though! But was it a dream or a flashback from my childhood - a demon from the past?

I remember our home habitually emitted eerie sounds; the floorboards creaked for no apparent reason, doors groaned, as if opened by an invisible hand and of course, Saturday nights!

On Saturday night our ritual would begin - comfortably seated around the 'Hellevision' in the ebony living room, armed with sweets, crisps and pop. It was horror night. My brothers; Stephen, Lance, Antonio and Matthew and I, the eldest and only girl (a blessing or a curse, depends on which side of the coin you're on!). We were all looking forward to our weekly appointment with Dracula.

My father was out as usual - with one of his so-called friends - who knows? Just before leaving the house, he would poke his head around the door into the living room, before repeating his weekly ceremonial chant, 'Make sure the back door is locked before you go to bed.' (In his deepest, bass voice, adding weight to his command.) He might as well have said leave all the windows and doors open for all we cared, we had mentally tuned out from the moment his head appeared around the door. Out of respect and fear of his authority, in unison we chorused, 'Yes Daddy.' The door bangs shut, he's gone now.

Our eyes are glued to the set, in anticipation. The spine-chilling tunes waft through the room, bringing with them the promise of a horror-filled night with Dracula . . . the air is electric as he approaches his virginal prey, who is unconscious of her doom! He arches forward, a long white neck extends towards the 'white rose' spread upon the bed. His mouth puckers in anticipation of his fleshly feast. I can feel my heart racing, vibrating like a drum against my chest, rising and falling rapidly like a plucked elastic band . . . Dracula exposes his menacing secret, concealed behind his lips - two-inch triangular pincers jut out from the sides of his mouth, ready to plunge into the smooth creamy jugular of his powerless victim.

I cast my eyes around the room - my brothers' eyes are protruding like golf balls, ready to pop into a hole; Stephen pretends not to be fazed by the grisly sight - but I'm sure he is in the process of wetting his pants! Matthew, the youngest, smothers his face with a cushion, rocking to and fro rapidly, his head beating rhythmically against the back of the floral settee. Lance and Antonio gasp and squeeze their eyes tightly shut! (They seem to see more of the back of their eyelids than Dracula.) However, this is the concoction of behaviours for the night, with a heady mix of fear and anticipation until, of course, Dracula meets his untimely end . . .

The screen lays blank before us. In my semi-conscious state I hear a melodious voice uttering, 'Thank you for watching, please remember to turn your sets off. Goodnight.' It dawns on me that our night has come to an end. I am fully awake now! The blackness of the room surrounds me, interrupted by the beams of light glimmering like stars from the scrambled screen. I jump up with lightning speed, flicking on the light switch and breathe a sigh of relief.

'It's time for bed!' I groan within as I look from one sibling to another. The task befalls me, yet again to awake them out of their slumber. 'Here we go!' muttering to myself, while shaking and pulling on their arms and legs. 'Wake up, get up, now! It's time for bed.'

By now, four pairs of eyes are fixed on me, rolling back and forth intermittently. You can see their thoughts written in their eyes. 'Are you gonna be first to venture into the dark passage?' The question looms in the cold air, suspended like a cloud above our heads. Nevertheless, this is an unavoidable obstacle en route to our rooms, and no one desires to be the *first* or the *last!*

Time

It's time! Time for what you say
Time! To set your life in order
Less distressing, caressing, harassing

Time to harness, direct and connect
Time to be all that you can be!

Time to believe in . . . me!
And all you've been gifted to be

Take a look on the inside!
It's waiting to come up - on the outside

What are you waiting for?

It's time to believe in . . . me!
And
All that I've been gifted to be!
Time to believe in me!

Dr Nevel Vassel

Ph.D, MA, B.Ed, Cert.Post Comp.Mgt, Dep.Agri.

Dr Vassel is a Course Director for MSc Multicultural Issues in Health and Social Care at the University of Central England in Birmingham, West Midlands. Also module leader for BSc Honours, Clinical Nursing Studies Option Module *'Issues In Multicultural Health Care'* and

BSc Hons. Palliative Care Option Module *'Issues in Multicultural Health Care'*.

He teaches Cultural Awareness on ENB Programmes, e.g. Diabetes, Mental Health, Tuberculosis, Intensive Care, Pain Management, Sickle Cell and Thalassaemia, Sexual Health Promotion and Renal Pathway. Dr Vassel specialises in Multicultural & Diversity Issues, Staff Training & Development and Leadership & Mentoring. He has 20 years of lecturing experience in Further and Higher Education institutions on a variety of courses such as Educational Management, Marketing Research, Educational Research Methods, Project Management, Proposal Writing, Project Management and Mentoring.

Dr Vassel gained his Doctor of Philosophy in Education (Ph.D) at the University of Manchester, his Master of Arts (MA) degree in Educational Management, and Bachelor of Education (B.Ed) at the University of Wolverhampton. His Ph.D study was based on Black Masculinity and Further Education Colleges in Britain and Jamaica.

He has conducted several seminars and workshops, which included presentations at University of Manchester in Staff Development and Training to Finnish clients focusing on *'Inequality Issues in Education'*, Trans-cultural Nursing Conference in London top titled *'Cultural Health Issues in Song and Verse'* and Royal College of Nursing, East Midland *Conference Mental Health Challenges in Multicultural Community.* Dr Vassel also presented at Black and Minority Ethnic Seminar, Lighthouse, Wolverhampton, on topic titled *'Multicultural and Partnership Education in Context'.* Furthermore he organises and runs workshops on Cultural Awareness on Diabetes, Mental Health, Sickle Cell, Equality and Inequality Practices in Care.

In addition Dr Vassel conducted Multicultural Health Awareness training sessions at North Birmingham High Croft Mental Health Hospital and for National Health Service (NHS) staff attending the University of Central England in Birmingham on short day release courses. He also did presentations on *Jamaican Cultural and Health Issues* to visiting College Nurse students from New York, USA, held at the University of Central England in Birmingham. At a national conference in Birmingham he was a speaker on the topic *Jamaican Language as Cultural Tool in Health and Social Care Settings.*

He was accredited as the first African Jamaican to research and grow Scotch Bonnet pepper in Britain. Dr Vassel appeared on British Television Channel 4 Grow Your Green Gardening series to explain his research activity. His recognition has been documented in Black Who's Who Book published by the New National and Caribbean Times. Dr Vassel is the cofounder of Cultural Training in Health, Education and Management (CTHEM) an enterprise that specialises in Cultural Awareness training for health care organisations, education, voluntary groups, companies and other establishments.

Dr Vassel is the author of two books of poems, titled *'Poems Calling Out'* and *'Poetic Vibes'*. He is the first African Jamaican Poet to have one of his poems, title *'The Journey'* to be permanently voiced, displayed in the City of Wolverhampton Museum. In addition he writes and presents short plays on cultural awareness in health care including mental health, diabetes, sickle cell and other problematic health issues.

Time For A Change

Come let we chat come let we rap
Come let we reason any time throughout the season

Come let we chat . . . it is about time
Of the things that we want to see go fine
Come let we set our goals and ambitions
For the sake of the future generation
Economical pressure is demanding
Environmental circumstances is dictating
Men and women find it difficult to get a job
Others can only think of sob, sob, sob

I searching for a that perfect opportunity
I reading that life is a living reality
I yearning for you and I to get together
To build and make this place much better
I powerful and strong like a lion
And valuable too like a ruff cut diamond
This time I will rise up like a raging sea
Ready to help everyone experiencing misery

Come let we chat come let we wrap
Come let we reason any time throughout the season

Come let we learn about race and ethnicity
Or go to an institution to improve illiteracy
Come let us spend a little time learning
How to care for the sick and dying
Rich or poor, life worth saving
Come let us talk about the environment and why it is hotting
Applying green education to add some cooling

Come let we chat come let we rap
Come let we reason any time throughout the season

Come let up reason about health and disease
How it is affecting our population please, please, please
Come let up discuss the evils of domestic violence
How children suffer this form of inconvenience
Let us talk about other concerns that really matters
Come let us do something before society goes to tatters
Come let us join and lend a helping hand
Pave a golden pathway for this lovely nation

Come let we chat come let we rap
Come let we reason any time throughout the season

Learning

Educators report that high numbers
Of youths are underachieving
Girls and boys it's flagrantly unbelieving
Others are grossly involved in drug taking
On the news a newly recruit end up dying

Her picture was shown on national TV
To inform you and me
That we have a sense of duty and responsibility
For the sake of this society

Unemployment figures are slowly coming down
Others are running around like a clown
Some find it difficult to drink tea from a cup
Others daze and craze and get flup

Teenage pregnancy is the latest fashion
Peer pressures increasing a drive toward this situation
Parents are simple and totally confused
This is not exciting so please don't be amused

It grand time to build some self-esteem
Smooth up your acts and come nicely clean
Education and learning is the only way out
Whether you live north, east, west or south

It time to get thinking radical Jean
Through tools of socio-cultural and political means
Daydreaming will not solve this problem
Group networking is the only way to solve them

How about stretching the volunteering philosophy
Increasing life-long learning via this opportunity
It offers access and participation
And encourages active collaboration

It prepares one to be the good leader
Put one in the framework of being a good feeder
Surely others will copy your actions
A good role model for the nation

Education is the key for KASH
It develop good knowledge, attitudes, skills, valuable habits
And all of that
So wherever in the world you may go
Volunteering decision is the seed you sow

Rasta Pickneys

The language of which I speak boldly
Is not for the heart weak coldly
Coming through Sheba Solomonic lines
Roots I represent throughout time and space

Rasta Pickney with the lion dread
Of its beauty I proudly display
Rasta Pickney with the lion dread
Viewers please don't be dismay

Nubian locks represent my identity
Bobo dread, natty dread is reality
Rising up with grace in a Babylon system
Do not really care for any skism

Land of my forefathers . . . Ethiopia calling
The place where civilisation start is still lasting
From biblical literature through to Herodotus
To medieval fantasy
I represent all things for humanity

Rasta Pickney with lion dreads
Of it beauty I proudly display
Rasta Pickney with lion dread
Viewers please don't be dismay

See I and I here . . . look!
See I and I there, look!
Respect I project. I self . . . I protect
Rasta is love . . . Rasta is you and I
Unified with a sense of purpose

Nevel Vassel

Grandma Eyes

Look into her eyes
you see love
Look into her eyes
you see warmth
Look into her face
you see history
Look into her heart
you see a story
Look at her hands
you see hardship
Look at her walk
there is rhythm
Look at her stance
you see command-ship

The love you see is based on love
The warmth you experienced is always welcoming
The face she poses represents our history
Her heart tells a story with honesty and integrity
Her hands share the revelation of many hours of hard labour
Working die cast machines on Pen Road

She walk upright with a rhythm
of reggae, ska, blue mento
To poco revival lick that make old boys
lick them tongue
She speak proudly of her children's
and grandchildren's achievements
Here and abroad and prays daily
their safety in a foreign land
But Mrs Eda Vassel
likes to smile
Wearing her glasses
Mr Veron

Glenis Williams

Glenis Williams was born and brought up in the West Midlands. Her parents came from Jamaica to the UK in the 1950s. Glenis graduated from university with a BA (Hons) degree in Media, Arts and Design. She is now actively involved in working with the community, with organisations co-ordinating cultural events and dealing with community development issues. She draws her inspiration for her creative writing from African Caribbean culture and experiences of growing up in a culturally diverse community.

Prejudice

We live here, we work here, and we breathe
Lives everywhere are full of joy, excitement, and new adventures
And of course there are many dreams.
Life can be full of sorrow, tragedy, death and disappointment
How bitter, how sweet life can be
Life goes on, and yes we still breathe.

We learn to crawl, we learn to speak
We learn to see further than the eye can reach
Reaction and interaction
The glance, the stares, the subtle body language
We all as humans understand
We see, we hear, we read
It speaks so clearly, there can be no mistake
It is loud, and it is strong
Making no apology for what it is, my name is prejudice and I belong.

The veil is draped from head to toe
It covers every crease and bow, trying hard to hide what's really there
The veil is shrouded with history,
Too powerful, to be tolerant of others
Too powerful, to share.

What was then, what is now, and certainly what could be
The veil is delicate; the veil is like steel, and very strong
The veil is real, as you and me.
It has taken me some years to see, the veil in others
And the veil I've built in me.
As life goes on, you will learn to see, the veil more clearly
You may be at work or out with friends
And if you watch very carefully
It will appear and you will see it very clear
The veil of prejudice is everywhere.

Black Reading Group

No50 Hadley Road

There, within the bricks and mortar, warmth, love and laughter. It seeps through the walls. The cluttered assembly of photos and things decorate the walls. The looking back, the good-time days, the memories of family and friends. The life here, the lives back home.

The front room never used, except on very special occasions when Pastor comes to visit, Christmas, christenings and birthdays. The dust and cobwebs cover the plastic sheets, as they lay draped on the furniture. The room is dead and lifeless and is only brought to life on these occasions.

The living room is a hive of activity, the colours, the smell, the buzz of conversation. The huge Brown Gram sits proud on the far side of the room like an aged old mammoth waiting. The printed pattern on the sofa, the printed patterns within the wallpaper, the pattern on the carpet, it's a carnival of colour. They fight amongst themselves.

Each chair stands rigid in its place, adorned with headrests crocheted with tender loving care, they stand stiff like candyfloss. Conversation and laughter bursts through loud and strong, the chit-chat of women in the kitchen and the deep raucous laughter of grown men. The sweet smell of Gramma's cooking drifts into every room, and leaves its lingering aroma. The kitchen is the heart of her home, where the chopping, the seasoning and the preparation takes place. The fish is frying, the dumplings are boiling, and the food is cooking. I can still smell thyme, pimento, garlic and herbs. Everyone is welcome, for there's always plenty to eat. The Dutch pot is never empty at number 50 Hadley Road.